D0031905

THREE HORSES

Roller Coaster Ride

A 4D BOOK

by Cari Meister

illustrated by Heather Burns

PICTURE WINDOW BOOKS
a capstone imprint

Three Horses is published by Picture Window Books,
A Capstone Imprint
1710 Roe Crest Drive
North Mankato, Minnesota 56003
www.mycapstone.com

Library of Congress Cataloging-in-Publication Data is available
on the Library of Congress website.
ISBN: 978-1-5158-2948-5 (library binding)
ISBN: 978-1-5158-2952-2 (paperback)
ISBN: 978-1-5158-2956-0 (eBook PDF)

Designer:
Lori Bye

Design elements by Shutterstock: Semiletava Hanna

Printed and bound in the USA
PA017

Download the Capstone app!

- Ask an adult to download the Capstone 4D app.

- Scan the cover and stars inside the book for additional content.

When you scan a spread, you'll find
fun extra stuff to go with this book!
You can also find these things
on the web at www.capstone4D.com
using the password: threehorses.29485

TABLE OF CONTENTS

CHAPTER 1

❧ ✵ ❧

The Barn Cat

Melody filled the bucket with soapy water. She set out a sponge, a comb, and some little purple rubber bands. Then she skipped down the barn aisle to get her pony.

"Let's braid your mane for the show tomorrow," Melody said as she reached Princess' stall. She leaned over and kissed Princess on her long nose.

Princess shook her head as the kiss landed on her nose. She stomped her hoof onto the ground. Slowly, she tried to nudge Melody out of the stall.

"Princess!" scolded Melody. "That was not very nice! Be a good pony. Follow me to the wash stall."

Melody yanked a little harder on the lead rope. Princess slowly moved forward.

"I can't believe it!" said Princess. "She's trying to get me to another horse show! Me! At a horse show! Doesn't she understand how silly she looks riding a cat?"

Sebastian, the draft horse from the next stall, looked at Princess. Nope. Nothing had changed. Princess was still a perfect palomino pony.

"But you see," Seb told the new barn dog Riley, "Princess doesn't believe she's a horse. She *thinks* she's a cat."

"Why?" asked Riley.

"From what I gather," said Seb, "when Princess was just a wee thing, her mother died. She was the only horse on the farm."

"How sad," replied Riley.

"One day a stray cat came into her stall and had kittens," continued Seb. "I guess she just became one of them."

"No wonder she is scared of me," said Riley. "You know—the cat and dog thing."

CHAPTER 2

❧ ✦ ❧

Tres Caballos Incognito

That night, Seb and Princess woke to loud kicking.

"Sebastian! Princess! Wake up!" called Snowy, the pony from two stalls down.

Seb blinked his eyes open.

"What is it?" asked Princess.

"It's time for *Tres Caballos Incognito,*" said Snowy.

Tres Caballos Incognito was the code name the trio used when they wanted to escape from the barn and go on exciting adventures.

Princess pawed in excitement. "Let's go! Do you have our disguises?" she asked.

"Right here," said Snowy, whipping out three fly masks. "We can put them on as soon as Sebastian gets us out of our stalls."

Seb was already standing in the aisle. "I'm ready for an adventure," he said.

"Me first!" said Princess. "Undo my latch! I MUST get out of here before the show tomorrow. I need to find someone to take these goofy horse braids out of my feline fur."

Seb clomped over to Princess' stall. He bent his long neck and opened her latch with his teeth.

"I think I know where to go to get your braids out," Seb said.

"You do?" asked Princess.

But before Seb could tell her more, Snowy stamped and cleared his throat. "Ahem!" he said. "Are you going to let me out?"

Seb clomped over to Snowy's stall. He looked down at the furry Shetland pony staring back at him.

"Thank you, my dear Sebastian," said Snowy. "If it were not for you letting me out, I would never have material for my novel *From the Horse's Mouth*. I'm grateful to you."

Sebastian blushed. "Thanks, Snowy," he said.

Snowy stamped. "PLEASE, Sebastian," he said. "You know how I dislike that childish name. Please call me by my show name—*The Blizzard*."

"Sorry about that, *The Blizzard*," said Seb. "I just forget sometimes."

"It's OK," said Snowy. "Just try to show some respect."

Seb nodded. He knew how important it was for Snowy to have a name that evoked power and strength.

After Snowy helped Seb and Princess with their masks, they were ready to leave.

But as they got closer to the door, they stopped short. The new guard dog was right in front of it.

CHAPTER 3

❖

The Guard Dog

"The dog!" cried Princess, skidding sideways, away from Riley.

"Shhh!" said Snowy. "He's asleep!"

Seb nodded toward the back door. "We should go that way," he whispered.

"Good idea," whispered Snowy. "Just let me grab my laptop."

Snowy pulled his laptop from behind its hiding spot.

All of a sudden Princess made a loud sound. To her it was a "MEOW!" To everyone else it was a snort.

"What is it?" asked Snowy.

"A mouse!" yelled Princess as she started chasing it.

The commotion woke Riley. He ran right toward Princess who forgot instantly about the mouse.

"The dog is going to eat me!" cried Princess.

Seb trotted between them.

Riley stopped barking.

"What are you all doing out of your stalls?" asked Riley.

"Going on an adventure," said Seb.

"Where?" asked Riley.

"We haven't decided yet," said Snowy. "I'm writing a novel and need more material."

Riley tilted his head. "You're writing a novel?" he asked. "How does that work?"

Snowy opened his laptop. He picked up a hoof pick with his lips. He typed each letter one by one with the hoof pick:

```
The ferocious dog showed his long,
sharp teeth.
```

"I see," said Riley. He was impressed. "Can I come with you?" he asked.

Princess gulped. She shook her head.

Snowy saw her displeasure. "You're needed here," he said. "You're the guard dog. I think you should stay."

Riley looked disappointed. "That's the worst word in the world," he said.

"What is?" asked Seb.

"Stay," said Riley. "Humans always tell dogs to stay. It's pretty mean if you think about it. *Stay* means 'I don't want you with me.' *Stay* means 'I'd rather leave you behind.' It's like a dagger to the soul," he said.

Snowy felt bad, but he knew it was not the right night to bring Riley along. "Perhaps next time," said Snowy.

That cheered Riley a bit, so he let them out the front door without waking Toni, the barn manager.

"Just be home by 6:00 a.m.," Riley called after them. "I don't want to get in trouble. I'm new here, and I want to stay on Toni's good side."

"Sure thing," said Snowy. "We'll be back by 6:00."

CHAPTER 4

✧

A Plan

The trio stepped into the night. Snowy took a deep breath and inhaled the smell of adventure.

"That went better than expected," said Seb. "With Riley and all."

Princess nodded. "It's weird," she said. "He didn't even try to eat me. Dogs don't usually like cats. Maybe he's not a *normal* dog."

Seb couldn't resist. "Or maybe," he said, "you're not a *normal* cat."

"What's that supposed to mean?" asked Princess. "Is it these braids? Oh Seb, you said you had an idea to get them out of my fur. What was your idea?"

"Oh right," said Seb. "I heard my owner Jane talking about a new spa for cats. It is called *Purrfectly Posh Felines*."

Princess' eyes lit up. "A spa for cats? That sounds wonderful!" she cried. "I bet they serve tuna on little pink plates. Oooh! Maybe they have velvet napping pillows. And catnip! And a play room full of mice!"

"I am not sure about all *that*," said Seb. "But I would bet they could take out your braids."

"PURRRfect!" said Princess.

Snowy opened up his laptop. He typed:

`Cat Spa.`

"Do you know where it is?" he asked.

Seb grinned. "Yes!" He said. "It's right next to the amusement park!"

Snowy knew why Seb was so excited. The amusement park would be deserted at night. What a perfect time for horses to visit!

"Did you know they just opened the new Loop-di-Loo?" asked Seb. "I overheard Jane telling Toni about the ride. It has a 400-foot drop and three loops! It sounds so fun!" Seb gulped, looking hopefully at Snowy. "Do you think you can run it?"

Snowy smiled. "Of course, dear Sebastian. After all, I have my computer. I am sure all of the instructions are on the Internet."

That put an extra kick in Seb's step. "Fantastic!" he said.

Snowy picked up the hoof pick and pecked out the words:

Amusement park.

Snowy looked up directions. "The spa and park are about 3 miles away," he said. "If we keep at a trot, we should be there by midnight. That means no stopping along the way."

"Well, let's go!" said Seb, trotting forward. "I can hardly wait!"

CHAPTER 5

❁

Closed!

It was about midnight when the trio arrived at *Purrfectly Posh Felines.* The spa was a mix between a fairy-tale gingerbread house and a modern resort.

"It looks purrfectly perfect!" shouted Princess from the road.

She ran up the steps, stopped to check her reflection in the window, and knocked.

Nobody came to the door.

Princess rang the bell.

Still no one.

She turned around and laughed nervously. "They must be tending to another kitty in back," she said.

Snowy joined her at the door.

"I'm sorry, Princess," he said. "The sign here says closed."

"Closed! What do you mean? How can it be closed?" asked Princess. "It's just after midnight. All cats are out and about now— hunting and what-not."

Princess banged on the door. "Open up! Open up!" she cried.

Snowy led her away. "Who is going to take out these braids?" she sobbed.

"We'll think of something," said Snowy. "Won't we, Seb?"

But Seb wasn't paying attention. He was staring at something in the distance. His body was alert. His eyes were wide. His tail was up. His whole body was shaking.

CHAPTER 6

On Duty

"What is it?" asked Snowy.

"Come quick!" said Seb.

"Is it a plastic bag flying in the wind?" asked Snowy. "If so, I prefer to stay here. Plastic bags are terrifying."

"No. It's not a plastic bag," said Seb.

"A dog?" asked Princess.

"No. It's bigger than that," answered Seb.

"A bear?" asked Snowy.

"No," said Seb. "Something much bigger."

"Bigger than a bear?" asked Princess. "Why would we want to come see it?"

"Because," said Seb. "It's the amusement park!"

"Oh!" said Snowy. "You should have said that. Let's go!"

The trio trotted toward the park.

"This is amazing!" said Seb. "I can't believe we are here. Look at the Loop-di-Loo! Look how tall it is! Look at all the other rides! This will surely be the best night ever!"

But when they got to the gate, they stopped.

"It's locked!" said Seb.

"A lock has never stopped us," said Snowy.

"C'mon Sebastian," said Princess. "I'm sure you can pick the lock."

"Well," said Seb studying the lock. "This one is different."

Just then, there was a loud HISSSS from behind a tree.

Princess spun around. "Look!" she said.

"A feline friend! How wonderful!"

Princess ran to the kitty and put her nose down. The kitty swatted at Princess' nose.

"Oww!" said Princess. "No need to swat at me. I'm your friend."

But the cat was in no mood for Princess. She dashed past *Tres Caballos Incognito* and climbed over the amusement park gate.

"Seb!" said Princess. "Open the gate! I want to follow my new friend! She probably knows where all the mice hide!"

"Friend?" asked Snowy. "It seemed to me that—"

"Hurry!" snapped Princess. "I might not be able to catch her."

Using his teeth, Sebastian fiddled with the lock.

"*Voila!*" he said, opening the gates. "Step right in!"

But once the three entered, they stopped. Sitting in a lighted booth, not far from the entrance, was a security guard.

Snowy stumbled and backed into a trash can.

CRASH!

The guard turned. "What was that?" he said.

But *Tres Caballos Incognito* had already galloped away.

They stopped near the Big Tamale—a giant boatlike ride that went upside down.

"Do you think he's coming this way?" asked Princess.

Snowy peeked around the corner.

"Yes!" he said. "Run!"

Snowy looked around. "Let's hide!" he said. "Follow me!"

Seb and Princess followed Snowy to the merry-go-round.

"Find a spot on the ride and stand completely still," he said. "Hurry. The guard is coming!"

CHAPTER 7

Still as Statues

The guard came from around the corner—right toward the merry-go-round.

"Be very still!" whispered Snowy.

The guard pointed his flashlight at the merry-go-round. His beam lit up Seb's big body.

Seb froze. He did not blink. He did not breathe. He was as still as a statue.

After what seemed like forever, the guard finally moved his light. "That's strange," he said. "I could have sworn I heard something over here."

The guard walked toward the Big Tamale. Seb let out a giant sigh.

"That was close!" said Princess.

"Let's go the other way," said Snowy. "We need to stay far away from that guard."

"Purrfect!" said Princess. "I think that's the way my tabby friend went."

Seb smiled. "And that's the way to the Loop-di-Loo!"

***

On the way to the Loop-di-Loo, Snowy stopped outside a funnel cake stand. He jumped over the counter and started mixing up funnel cakes. "I'm starving," he said. "Let's eat."

"You know how to make those?" asked Seb.

"How hard can it be?" asked Snowy. "You throw in some mix, oil, and water. Then you cook it. Princess, please plug in the machine."

But Princess did not plug in the machine. She was not there. Princess had found the kitty and was trying very hard to be friends.

The kitty wasn't sure what to think of Princess, but decided she was not a threat. If this silly pony wanted to follow her around, that seemed OK.

Back at the funnel cake stand, Seb and Snowy had figured out the machine. They were up to their eyeballs in funnel cakes!

They ate as many as they could.

"These are delicious!" said Seb, "But I am stuffed now!"

"Me too!" said Snowy. "Ready for the Loop-di-Loo?"

Seb nodded. "Let's go."

CHAPTER 8

❖

The Loop-di-Loo

On the way to the ride, Snowy read up on how to run it. "It's easy," he said. "You get in, I push the start button, and the ride is off!"

Seb was so excited he bolted up the entrance ramp. "I can't believe it!" he said. "I'm finally going on a roller coaster. I've dreamed about this day for so long!"

Seb trotted over to the front car. He tried to get in. But there was a problem. Only his front legs fit. He walked a step, but then only his back legs were in. He went back and forth, but it was no use.

"I'm too big!" he cried. "I don't fit!"

Snowy studied the situation, but came to the same conclusion.

"I'm sorry," said Snowy. "I'm afraid you're right. Let's go find another ride where you can fit."

"But I wanted to ride this ride!" said Seb, falling to the ground. "That was the plan!"

"I understand," said Snowy. "But sometimes plans have to change. The sooner you can get over it, the more fun you will have."

Seb stood up. Snowy was right. The night was not over. And there were more rides at the park. They started walking down the exit ramp when Seb had an idea.

"Snowy?" he asked.

"Yes?"

"Will you ride the Loop-di-Loo for me and tell me all about it? It will almost be as good as if I was riding it."

Snowy's eyes grew wide. "I don't know," he said. "I love adventures—like exploring new places—but I am NOT a thrill-seeker. There is a BIG difference."

"Plus," said Snowy patting his tummy.
"I am very full from all those funnel cakes."

Seb pleaded with his big brown eyes.

"OK," said Snowy getting into the front
seat. "Just this once. Go over there and push
the green button."

Snowy closed his eyes as the car clicked
up the first hill. He took a deep breath.

"NEIGHHHHH!" he screamed as the car
rocketed through the first loop.

The second loop was bigger and even scarier.

By the third loop, Snowy was in shock. His tummy felt awful and could not be ignored. He pawed at it. He wished horses could throw up like other animals, but he knew that was not possible. Poor Snowy had to do the only thing he could to make himself feel better.

***

When the car got back to the station, Snowy stepped out quickly.

Seb noticed the steaming pile on the floor.

"Snowy?" he asked "Do you think we should clean that up?"

Snowy nodded, then ran down the exit ramp.

"Please never ask me to do that again," he said.

Seb chuckled to himself. He found a
dustpan. He scooped the poop and put
it under a bush. Then he caught up with
Snowy. "So was it fun?"

"That is not a word I would use," said
Snowy. "Now let's find something YOU
can ride."

CHAPTER 9

❧ ❀ ☙

The Big Tamale

The Big Tamale was the perfect ride for Seb. There were big long row seats. Seb had no problem getting in.

"Ready?" asked Snowy.

"Ready!" said Seb. "Hit it!"

Snowy pushed the green "go" button just as he saw Princess galloping toward him. She was crying.

"What's the matter?" he asked.

"My new friend—the tabby kitty—she deserted me! We hadn't even found any mice yet."

Snowy patted her on the shoulder. "It's OK, Princess. Some cats are just that way. But don't worry. You still have us."

Princess sniffed.

The Big Tamale was making a swoop down toward them.

Whoosh!

"Hi, Princess!" shouted Seb.

Princess nodded and watched.

The Big Tamale came down again. This time a little closer.

SWOOOSH!

"Come ride with me!" shouted Seb.

Snowy stopped the ride and Princess got into the Big Tamale with Seb. As they swooshed around, her braids fell out.

"Princess, your braids!" said Snowy when the ride came to a halt. "See? I told you we would think of something!"

Princess and Seb rode three more rides. But their fun soon came to an end when the guard spotted them on the security camera.

"What on earth?" he said.

Luckily, Snowy saw him coming. By the time the guard got to the ride, all three horses were standing in the grass eating.

The guard scratched his head. "What a very strange night," he said.

***

The next morning as Toni was watching the news, she dropped her donut.

"I can't believe it!" she said. "They got out again! And they went all the way to the amusement park?"

Riley barked. Toni reached down to pet him. "What happened, Riley?" she asked. "You are supposed to be a guard dog."

Riley looked up at her with the donut in his mouth.

Toni laughed. "Good thing I like you, or I might get mad."

Riley rolled over so Toni could rub his belly.

"Come on, you goofy dog," she said. "Let's hook up the trailer and go to the amusement park."

***

Tres Caballos returned to Farley Farms right as Melody arrived. She was dressed for the show.

"What's going on?" she asked.

Toni started to explain, but Princess pushed past Seb and Snowy and rushed to Melody's side. She put her head on Melody and nickered.

Melody patted Princess on the neck. "There, there," she said. "It looks like you've had a rough night. And your mane! What happened to your braids? And that scratch on your nose? Where did you get that?"

Melody stroked Princess and cooed soft words. "I'm just glad you're all right," she said. As Melody led Princess back to her stall, she said "I don't think we should go to the show today."

Princess turned back to Seb and Snowy and smiled.

That night, while everyone was asleep, Snowy picked up his hoof pick and began typing part of his novel:

```
Try as he might, our hero could not
contain himself. His belly hurt. The sky
was spinning. He was embarrassed by his
accident. But like all good heroes,
he did not let his setback stand in his
way. He went on to help his friends have
the adventure of a lifetime.
```

GLOSSARY

commotion—a lot of noisy, excited activity

conclusion—a decision or realization based on the facts that you have

desert—to leave someone

disguise—clothing that hides you by making you look like something else

embarrass—to feel silly or foolish in front of others

feline—any animal of the cat family

plead—to beg someone to do something

shock—a mental or emotional upset caused by an event

threat—something that can be considered dangerous

thrill-seeker—a person who does dangerous things to feel pleasure and excitement

ABOUT THE AUTHOR

Cari Meister has written more than 130 books for children, including the Tiny series (Penguin) and the Fast Forward Fairy Tales series (Scholastic). Cari is a school librarian and she loves to visit other schools and libraries to talk about the joy of reading and writing. Cari lives in the mountains of Colorado with her husband, four boys, one horse, and one dog.

ABOUT THE ILLUSTRATOR

Heather Burns is an illustrator from a small town called Uttoxeter in the UK. In 2013, she graduated from the University of Lincoln with a degree in illustration and has been working as a freelance illustrator ever since. Heather has a passion for bringing stories to life with pictures and hopes that her work makes people smile. When she's not working she's usually out walking her grumpy black Labrador, Meadow!

TALK ABOUT IT

1. Why do you think it was so important for Seb to go on the Loop-di-Loo?

2. If Riley the guard dog had come with *Tres Caballos Incognitos*, how would this story be different?

3. Name three ways *Tres Caballos Incognitos* supported each other in the story.

WRITE ABOUT IT

1. Write a scene from the point of view of the amusement park security guard. What does he see? What is he thinking?

2. Snowy likes to be called by his show name, The Blizzard. Write about a time when people called you something you didn't like.

3. Each member of *Tres Caballos Incognitos* has a secret dream. Write about a dream of your own.

BOOKS IN THE THREE HORSES SERIES

THE FUN DOESN'T STOP HERE!